For Helen. And a big
thank you to Adélie
for her help.

Nosy Crow and its logos are trademarks of Nosy Crow, Ltd. Used under license.

First U.S. edition 2014

Library of Congress Catalog Card Number 2013943092

ISBN 978-0-7636-7068-9

13 14 15 16 17 18 FGF 10 9 8 7 6 5 4 3 2 1

Printed in Shenzhen, Guangdong, China

This book was typeset in Goudy Infant.
The illustrations were done in gouache.

Nosy Crow
An imprint of
Candlewick Press
99 Dover Street
Somerville, Massachusetts 02144

www.nosycrow.com
www.candlewick.com

Pip and Posy
The Bedtime Frog

Axel Scheffler

nosy™
crow

An imprint of Candlewick Press

Posy was going to
sleep over at Pip's house.

She packed her suitcase very carefully.
She didn't want to forget anything.

Then she got on the bus.

Pip was very happy
to see Posy.
"Hi, Posy!" he called.

"Hello, Pip!" Posy said.

Pip and Posy had lots of fun.
They played with cars.

They played with the farm.

And then they played
Pirates in the Hospital.

They ate
spaghetti.

They had a
bubble bath.

They brushed
their teeth.

And they read
a funny story.
After that, it was
time for bed.

"Night-night, Posy," said Pip
as he cuddled up with his piggy.

"Sweet dreams, Pip," said Posy.

Pip was almost asleep when he heard a voice say "Froggy!"

It was Posy.
"I've forgotten Froggy," she cried.

"I can't sleep without Froggy!"

Pip turned his light on.
"Would you like this teddy bear?" he said.

But Posy didn't want Pip's teddy bear.
"It's not green," she said.
"My frog is green."

"Would you like my dinosaur?" said Pip.
"He's green."

"No!" said Posy.
"He's too big and too scary!"

"What about my frog
bank?" said Pip.

"No!" said Posy.
"That is the *wrong frog*!"

Posy cried and cried and cried.

Oh, dear!

Pip thought for a moment.
Then he did a **very difficult** thing.

"Would you like Piggy, Posy?" he said.

Posy stopped crying.
Piggy was a very nice pig.

"Yes, please, Pip," she said.

Soon Pip was asleep.

And so was Posy.

And the next day, when Posy
got home,
she found her frog . . .

and gave him
a big hug.

Hooray!